The Blue Bird

Written and illustrated by

FIONA FRENCH

NEW YORK HENRY Z. WALCK, INC.

© Fiona French, 1972. ISBN: 0-8098-1194-4. LC: 79-188900. Printed in Holland.

There was once a young scholar called Chiang Ti. He lived in China and his house stood on the edge of a lake. In the summer he could hear the birds singing while he sat studying his books.

In the house next door there lived a family who had a daughter, and her name was Jade Lotus. Now Jade Lotus had a beautiful

blue bird which she kept in a cage. One day the bird stopped singing. Jade Lotus called to Chiang Ti and said to him, "Can you hear how quiet it is today? My bird has stopped singing."

The bird inside the cage gazed mournfully at them; he would not sing and he would not eat. Chiang Ti looked in his books but could not find a cure for the illness. Then he said, "I have heard about an Enchantress who lives in a

palace not far away. People say she can speak to birds and understands what they say." So Chiang Ti and Jade Lotus set out to find the Enchantress, and took the bird in the cage with them.

They had only gone a few steps when they saw a tortoise lying helplessly on its back.

"I was trying to reach some juicy leaves when I fell over," the tortoise said.

Chiang Ti kindly put him on his feet.

"Where are you going?" asked the tortoise.
"To see the Enchantress," they said.
"Then I will come too."
So Chiang Ti carried the tortoise under his arm, and they went
on their way.

A little farther on they heard an odd noise, and saw a cat sitting on a rock in the middle of the lake. He was singing sadly to himself.

"Please would you help me off this rock," he called.

Chiang Ti gladly took off his shoes and waded into the water.

The cat climbed on to his back.
"Where are you going?" asked the cat.
"We are going to the Enchantress," they said.
"Then I will come too."
And he curled round Chiang Ti's neck, and fell asleep.

The animals were too heavy to carry for long so Chiang Ti and Jade Lotus sat down for a rest.

They saw a cloud in the sky and watched in surprise as it changed into a rain dragon. He looked very fierce, but he had a gentle voice. He was a lonely rain dragon, all by himself.

"Where are you going?" he asked.
"We are going to see the Enchantress," they said.
"In that case I will come too."
So Chiang Ti and Jade Lotus set off again, and the rain dragon
followed them all the way to the palace.

The palace was high, and towered above them.
The roofs and walls were covered with stone birds.
Everything was very quiet. They opened the door and went inside.

Thousands of birds were carved into the pillars and woven into the screens and carpets, but they did not make a sound, their wings did not move. They were frozen still.

Then Chiang Ti and Jade Lotus saw the Enchantress—and suddenly they too were almost frozen with fear.

But they bravely went up to her, seeking help for their bird.

When the Enchantress saw the bird in the cage her eyes lit up.

She spoke in a sharp, piercing voice.
"Give me that bird."
Chiang Ti and Jade Lotus shrank back in terror.
"Give me that bird," screamed the Enchantress.
Black, angry clouds rolled out of the sky.
"Give me that bird, or the storm will destroy you," cried the
Enchantress.

The threatening storm clouds gathered over the palace.
The Enchantress shrieked, "All the birds in the world must be mine. I will turn them to stone and there will be no more singing."
Jade Lotus and Chiang Ti huddled together, and tried to hide the bird from her.

"I will help you. Don't worry," said the tortoise.
He began to grow. He grew and grew until his shell was like a mountain.

The tortoise held up the storm clouds on his back, and all their fury faded away.
The Enchantress spread her wings, and flew at the tortoise.

Up sprang the cat, enormous and fierce.
He caught the Enchantress in his paws,
and ate her up in one mouthful.

"Now there is one thing left for me to do," said the rain dragon. "I will wash away the evil which the Enchantress made."
He turned himself into a shower of rain. As the drops of water touched the stone birds on the roofs and walls, they woke up, shook their wings and began to sing. One by one, they flew away. Chiang Ti and Jade Lotus watched in amazement as the whole palace disappeared.

The blue bird inside his cage flew up and down shaking his wings as if trying to escape.

"If I set him free perhaps he will sing again, too," said Jade Lotus. So she opened the cage door, and they watched him as he flew away. Suddenly they heard him singing a song.

"Tui, tui."

Over and over again he sang the song.

"Tui, tui."

It echoed through the countryside.

"Tui, tui."

And it followed them all the way home. "Tui, tui."

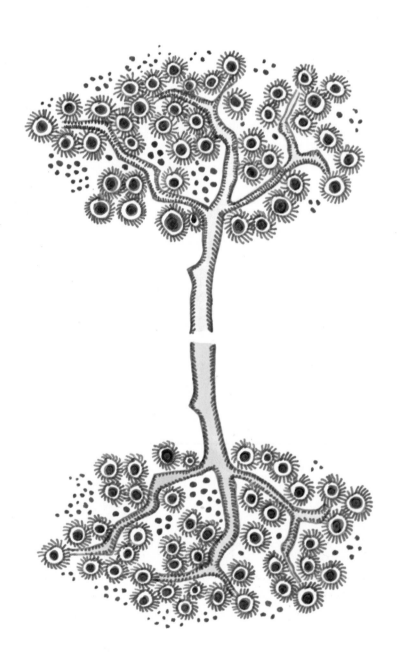